This book is dedicated to Beavers, who are the fastest and the best builders in the world; and especially to the new Beavers of Scotland, who have just moved back in after many years away. Good luck, Beavers!

First U.S. edition 2011

Library of Congress Cataloging-in-Publication Data

Moore, Inga.
A house in the woods / Inga Moore. — 1st U.S. ed.
p.   cm.
Summary: Two Little Pigs whose small homes in the woods have been accidentally destroyed by Bear and Moose decide to build a house they can all share, and with the help of Beaver Builders they soon have a fine new home.
ISBN 978-0-7636-5277-7
[1. House construction—Fiction. 2. Building—Fiction. 3. Friendship—Fiction. 4. Forest animals—Fiction.]   I. Title.
PZ7.M7846Hou 2011
[E]—dc22   2010050827

SCP 16 15 14 13 12 11
10 9 8 7 6 5 4 3 2 1

Printed in Humen, Dongguan, China

This book was typeset in Clarendon. The illustrations were done in pencil, pastel, and wash.

Candlewick Press, 99 Dover Street, Somerville, Massachusetts 02144

visit us at www.candlewick.com

A House in the Woods

INGA MOORE

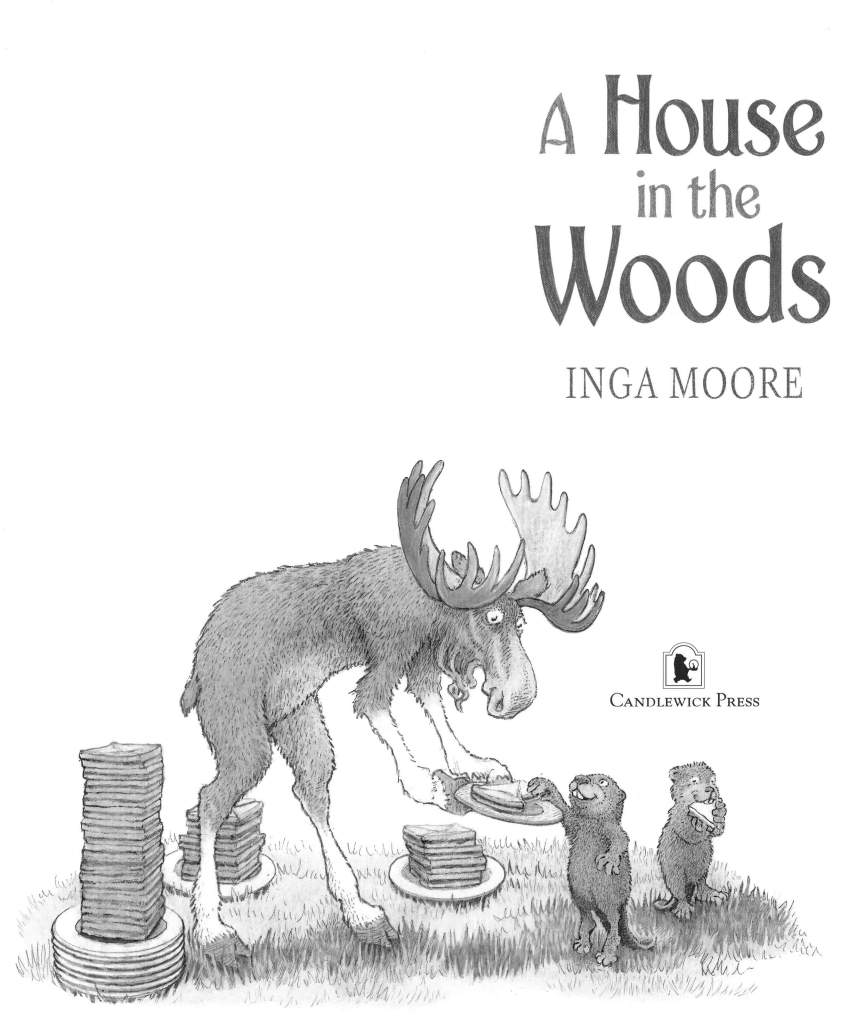

CANDLEWICK PRESS

A Little Pig had made a den for herself
in the woods. Next door, another Little Pig
had made himself a hut.

One morning the two Little Pigs
went out walking together.
One Little Pig found a feather,
and the other found an
interesting stick.

But when the first Little Pig brought her feather
home to her den, she discovered that Bear had moved in—
which she didn't mind, because she liked Bear.

But Bear was so big that—oh, dear!—
the den was wrecked.

And when the second Little Pig went home to his hut with his stick, he discovered that Moose had moved in — which he didn't mind either, because he liked Moose.

But Moose was even bigger than Bear, and when he stood up politely to say good morning — *CRASH!* — the hut was also wrecked.

Which left the two Little Pigs with nowhere
to live—not to mention Moose and Bear.
This was a pickle. It really was.

Then Moose had a brilliant idea: Why not build
a big house where they could all live together?

Well, *that* was a good idea!
Except that building a big house
with real windows and doors,
a roof, stairs, and chimney stacks
isn't easy. They couldn't do it
on their own.

So Moose called the Beavers
on the telephone . . .

and soon afterward a team of Beaver Builders
came to help them.

The Beavers said that they wished
to be paid in peanut-butter sandwiches.
No one had any objection.

So they felled the timber . . .

and the work began.

By lunchtime the walls
of the house were up . . .

and by dinnertime the roof
was on. (The lunch and dinner
times were on different
days, of course. Beavers are
fast, but not that fast.)

Bear made the staircases and
chimney stacks, while Moose
fitted the windows and doors.

Then they both went with the two Little Pigs
to the junkyard for furniture and curtains
and all the other things that go inside a house.

At last the house was finished.

The Beavers handed over their bill and left.

There was just enough time to get to the store . . .

to buy the bread and peanut butter.

Then the Little Pigs helped Moose and Bear
make six plates of peanut-butter sandwiches,

which they delivered in person to the Beavers,
who had all gone back to their lodge on the lake.

It had been a busy time
for the Little Pigs and
Moose and Bear.

They had worked hard.

Had it been worth it?

What do you think?

Just look!
What a beautiful new
house they have!

Bear went to bed first
because she was so tired.
And after they had finished
their supper and washed
the dishes . . .

and told stories for a while around the fire,

Moose and the two Little Pigs climbed the stairs to bed.

Soon the only sounds to be
heard were the soft cheeps
of sleepy birds roosting
in the rafters, the tiny
rustling of wood mice in
the fallen leaves outside,
and, just now and then,
the gentle snoring of Bear.

Good night, Bear.
Good night, Moose.
Good night, Little Pigs.

Sweet dreams, everyone!